Dear Parents,

Welcome to the Scholastic Reader series. We have taken more than 80 years of experience with teachers, parents, and children and put it into a program that is designed to match your child's interests and skills.

Level 1—Short sentences and stories made up of words kids can sound out using their phonics skills and words that are important to remember.

Level 2—Longer sentences and stories with words kids need to know and new "big" words that they will want to know.

Level 3—From sentences to paragraphs to longer stories, these books have large "chunks" of texts and are made up of a rich vocabulary.

Level 4—First chapter books with more words and fewer pictures.

It is important that children learn to read well enough to succeed in school and beyond. Here are ideas for reading this book with your child:

- Look at the book together. Encourage your child to read the title and make a prediction about the story.
- Read the book together. Encourage your child to sound out words when appropriate. When your child struggles, you can help by providing the word.
- Encourage your child to retell the story. This is a great way to check for comprehension.
- Have your child take the fluency test on the last page to check progress.

Scholastic Readers are designed to support your child's efforts to learn how to read at every age and every stage. Enjoy helping your child learn to read and love to read.

— Francie Alexander
Chief Education Officer
Scholastic Education

To my school chums—Matt, Larry, and Alan
—G. M.

To Jeremy
—R. B.

Text copyright © 2005 by Grace Maccarone.
Illustrations copyright © 2005 by Rick Brown.
Activities copyright © 2006 by Scholastic Inc.
All rights reserved. Published by Scholastic Inc.
SCHOLASTIC, CARTWHEEL BOOKS, FIRST-GRADE FRIENDS, and associated logos
are trademarks and/or registered trademarks of Scholastic Inc.

Library of Congress Cataloging-in-Publication Data is available.

ISBN 0-439-83298-5

12 11 10 9 8 7 6 5 4 3 2   6 7 8 9 10/0
Printed in the U.S.A. • This edition first printing, May 2006

GRADUATION DAY IS HERE!

by **Grace Maccarone**

Illustrated by **Rick Brown**

Scholastic Reader — Level 1

SCHOLASTIC INC.

New York Toronto London Auckland Sydney
Mexico City New Delhi Hong Kong Buenos Aires

Sam wears a shirt.
Sam wears a tie.

Sam wears nice pants.
And this is why.

Sam learned so much
at school this year.

Now Graduation Day
is here!

Sam has a robe.
Sam has a hat.

Sam puts them on.
The hat is flat.

Sam's mom and brother
have to wait.

"Let's go," says Mom.
"We can't be late!"

Sam asks,
"Where's Dad?"

"You'll see him soon,"
Mom says. "He'll meet us
there at noon."

The chairs are set up
on the grass.

Sam runs to sit
among his class.

But Dad isn't here!
It's 12:01.
The Pledge of Allegiance
has begun.

At 12:01,
Sam is sad.

At 12:02,
Sam sees Dad.

At 12:02,
Sam is glad.

Now the children
sing out loud.

All the moms and dads
are proud.

Sam and his class
walk single file.

The teacher shakes
Sam's hand and smiles.

"You've learned to read and write and spell," she says. "Good job! You have done well."

Now grandmas, grandpas,
moms, and dads
hug and kiss
the brand-new grads.

And after graduation ends,
Sam goes to lunch
with all his friends.